A DREAM VACATION

For my grandson Josef
C.J.H.

For my wife Cheryl
who makes dreams come true
R.M.

With special thanks to Sam Keiser.

A Dream Vacation

Written by Carol J. Haile
Illustrated by Robert Miller

Book Design by Carol J. Haile and Robert Miller
Copyright 2003 by Carol J. Haile and Robert Miller

FIRST EDITION

Library of Congress Control Number: 2002116542

Panda Bear Press
P.O. Box 6892
Wyomissing, PA 19610-0892
USA

ISBN 0-9724699-0-7

Printed and bound in USA

A DREAM VACATION

By Carol J. Haile

Illustrated by Robert Miller

Panda Bear Press
2003

"Please, Grandma, tell us again how you met Noah! Tell us again, *please*, about your dream vacation!"

Grandma Panda smiled as she removed a tray of cookies from the oven. "Well, just one more time...."

Little panda feet scurried to the living room. Samantha took her usual place on the floor to the right of the rocking chair, and Benjamin sat on the left. Several of the younger pandas crowded near the bowl of fresh bamboo. Grandpa Joe filled it every morning with tender, tasty leaves he picked from his carefully manicured garden.

Grandma sat down and covered her legs with a warm afghan. "Well now, where should I begin?"

She paused briefly and began to tell her story.

"Many years ago, Grandpa and I got married and set up housekeeping in the north end of the forest. While Grandpa Joe was hard at work collecting bamboo, I was busy tidying the treehouse and inviting neighbors over for tea."

Back then, before the flood, bamboo was getting harder to find. Grandpa Joe worked longer and longer hours and was home less and less. We treasured the little bit of time we could spend together.

We disagreed very rarely, and then *only* when we discussed our vacation.

I would say,
> "I want a vacation with lots to do,
> And to have a good time doing fun things with you —
> To laugh much, make friends, to play in the sun,
> I want a vacation that's full of fun!"

And Grandpa Joe would insist,
> "But I work so hard all day up in the trees,
> I want a vacation to sleep when I please........"

His voice usually trailed off to a whisper. I rarely heard the end of his little poem. Grandpa was always so tired at the end of his long day at work. Conditions in the forest made his job more difficult all the time, but he never talked about it. Grandpa said he didn't want me to worry.

He really needed a break, and we decided to take a vacation very soon!

We visited The Busy Bee Travel Agency to see if we could find a perfect vacation, one that would make both of us happy. Honey Bee, the travel agent, suggested we sign up for a seven-day, ten-city tour. The schedule included lots of sightseeing, concerts and parties. I was so excited I wanted to hurry home and pack!

Unfortunately, Grandpa Joe noticed there was no time on the busy schedule for him to relax and nap. "Well," Honey Bee said, "this is certainly not the vacation to take if you want to relax!"

She suggested we rent a secluded cabin in the mountains. Grandpa Joe liked this idea very much. He could catch up on his sleep, dozing every day in the cool, clean mountain air.

Now I was quite unhappy. There would be no neighbors to meet, no one to invite over for tea, no parties. While Grandpa slept, what was I to do? "Well," Honey Bee buzzed, "this is certainly not the vacation to take if you want to socialize!"

Grandpa and I were disappointed but not discouraged! We knew we would find our perfect vacation if we just kept looking.

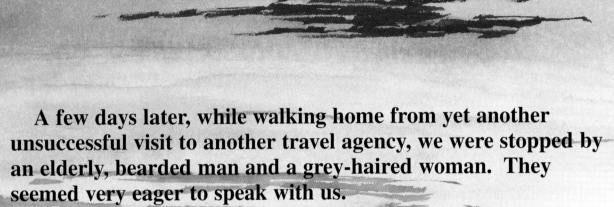

A few days later, while walking home from yet another unsuccessful visit to another travel agency, we were stopped by an elderly, bearded man and a grey-haired woman. They seemed very eager to speak with us.

The gentleman introduced himself, "Hello, my name is Noah and this is my wife. I would like you to take an exciting journey with us."

An exciting journey! Noah had our full attention and we listened very closely.

"God told me it will rain for forty days and forty nights," he said. "Very soon, a flood will cover the entire earth. I have built an Ark to save us.

"There is only enough room on the Ark for one male and one female of every animal on the earth. When the flood is over, all the animals who have made the long journey will be rewarded with a fresh, clean new world in which to live.

"You, Joe and Amanda, are the pandas I want to take with me on the Ark! But we must leave *now*. *Please* say you will come."

I thought the story Noah told us was very strange. Imagine, a great flood washing the entire earth, in much the same way I cleaned the floor of the treehouse by pouring a bucket of water over it once a week!

Grandpa Joe surprised me. He stood straight and tall and spoke with a firm, serious tone.

"In my youth I played in lush, green trees
Which struggle now to grow and breathe.
The freshwater lakes that sparkled each dawn
Have withered and dried — and many are gone."

Then he added,

"This is about the fate of all pandas —
Our vacation will have to wait, Amanda!
The problems the rain forests have are severe,
We *must* board the Ark, our duty is clear!"

I hadn't realized how strongly your grandfather felt about all
the problems in the forest until Noah started talking to us.
It was clear that Grandpa was determined to take this trip.
I smiled, looked at him, and said,

"I'll spend lots of time on this journey with you —
Something I dearly want to do.
This trip sounds like it just might be
A lot of fun for you and me!"

"There's no time to waste!" exclaimed Mrs. Noah. "Follow
me, and don't worry! Everything you will need is already on
the Ark."

Grandpa and I hurried along. In the distance we saw a long line of animals already marching two by two — two elephants, two giraffes, two gorillas, two crocodiles, two rabbits, and many other strange animals we had never seen before. Some slithered along, some strutted, some hopped.

The air was alive with birds flying by — parrots wearing feathers of fluorescent green, owls with enormous eyes, anxious hummingbirds zig-zagging through the air.

Soon, we joined the other animals in line. "Hello, I'm Orville." "I'm Olivia," said the tall Ostriches.

"Hello, I'm Leonard." "My name is Lizzy," said the regal Lions.

We were too busy making introductions to notice we were nearing the Ark. Suddenly, there it was! We gasped! It was *huge*, so much larger than the boats pictured on the posters hanging on the walls of the travel agencies we had visited.

ATTENTION......

As soon as Grandpa Joe and I entered the Ark, we were shown to our quarters. Grandpa smiled as he climbed into the roomy hammock in the corner of the room. It was a good time for a nap!

I started preparing a list of my many new friends. I would first invite Anthony and Andrea Anteater to a tea party in the large social room down the hall. Then I would invite the Bears, then the Crocodiles, then the Deer....

Over the loudspeaker, Mrs. Noah said, "Welcome aboard Noah's Ark! There are just a few things you should know. Mr. and Mrs. Canary prefer not to sit beside the Cats in the dining hall. For the comfort and safety of all passengers, Mr. and Mrs. Porcupine have decided to dine alone. Finally, please, *please* don't upset Mr. and Mrs. Skunk!"

I looked up from my list. Of course, Skunks would be on the Ark! Grandpa Joe looked over from his hammock, chuckled, and then resumed his nap. I tried to remember which couple should I put next on my invitation list, the Goats or the Geckos?

Crash! The massive doors of the Ark closed and the walls shuddered. Just as Noah had said, it began to rain, but not just a regular, everyday rain. *Big* buckets of rain poured down from the sky, enough to wash the entire earth!

In a few days, the flood waters rose and the Ark began to float.

Grandpa, happily settled in his comfortable hammock,
sipped tall glasses of spring water as he relaxed and napped.
He enjoyed the rocking back and forth of the Ark as the heavy
waters and pounding rains shook the thick wooden hull.

Meanwhile, I went to work inviting all my new friends to tea. I prepared tasty sunflower seed biscuits for Curtis and Cathy Cardinal's party. When I invited the Gazelles, I remembered to set out an attractive assortment of wafers made of grass and hay.

I'm proud to say that everyone looked forward to receiving one of my invitations. As my popularity as a hostess grew, Noah and Mrs. Noah encouraged me to plan larger and more elaborate events.

When I held a fashion show, I had no idea it would be such a smashing success! Flossie and Freddie Flamingo showed off their beautiful, pink plumes. The very stylish black-spotted yellow coats worn by the Leopards brought lots of 'oohs' and 'ahhs' from the crowd.

The real show-stopper was the shiny armor proudly worn by Arnold and Annie Armadillo. When Arnold demonstrated the protective qualities of his coat by curling up in a tight ball, the crowd cheered!

'Talent Night' soon became a regular event aboard the Ark. Milton and Martha Monkey were so funny when they sang silly songs! Bob and Betty Bat wowed the audience by hanging upside down on the ceiling. Seymour and Susie Skunk performed clever little dance routines.

Sometimes, Susie tripped over Seymour's tail, but it didn't matter. The audience always gave them a generous round of applause. After all, nobody wanted to upset the Skunks.

FINISH LINE

FIRST PLACE

On Day Forty the rain finally stopped, and Grandpa Joe happily helped me organize the races every afternoon on the sunny top deck. He usually rooted for Harry and Henrietta Horse. They frequently crossed the finish line first when they raced against the Yaks and Kangaroos.

I was always very careful to make sure everyone had an equal chance to win. However, when Seymour and Susie Skunk raced, I assigned Tommy and Teresa Turtle as their competition. The Skunks won every time, of course, but the Turtles didn't mind. Nobody wanted to anger the Skunks.

Occasionally, Grandpa Joe would climb to the highest roof of the Ark to enjoy a most spectacular view of the sparkling water. He sometimes spent the entire afternoon watching the peaceful motion of the gentle waves.

One afternoon, from his seat on the roof, Grandpa saw something moving in the distant sky. It approached, fluttering. Was it?.....Yes! It was a white dove! Others saw the dove too, and soon a curious crowd gathered on deck. Noah, especially, seemed very anxious.

The dove landed on the Ark. She carried an olive branch in her beak. "Land!" Noah shouted. "The earth is becoming green again! Our journey will soon be over!"

The Chipmunks scurried from deck to deck announcing the news.

"Soon we will again sip nectar from the ruby red flowers on a trumpet vine," said the Hummingbirds.

"Soon we will again feel the wind in our manes as we run free across the wide open fields," said the Horses.

And Grandpa Joe added,
"Soon I will climb trees lush and green,
Sip water from pools that are clear and clean,
Breathe air that is crisp and sweet and new,
See bountiful harvests of fresh bamboo."

The celebration that night lasted well into the early hours of the next morning. So much laughter, so much singing, so much dancing! The moment was also bittersweet. Soon, I would be saying good-bye to all my wonderful, new friends.

As the first light of the new day peeked over the horizon, Grandpa Joe and I quietly strolled down the long, wide deck of the Ark. We paused to look up at the soft morning sky.

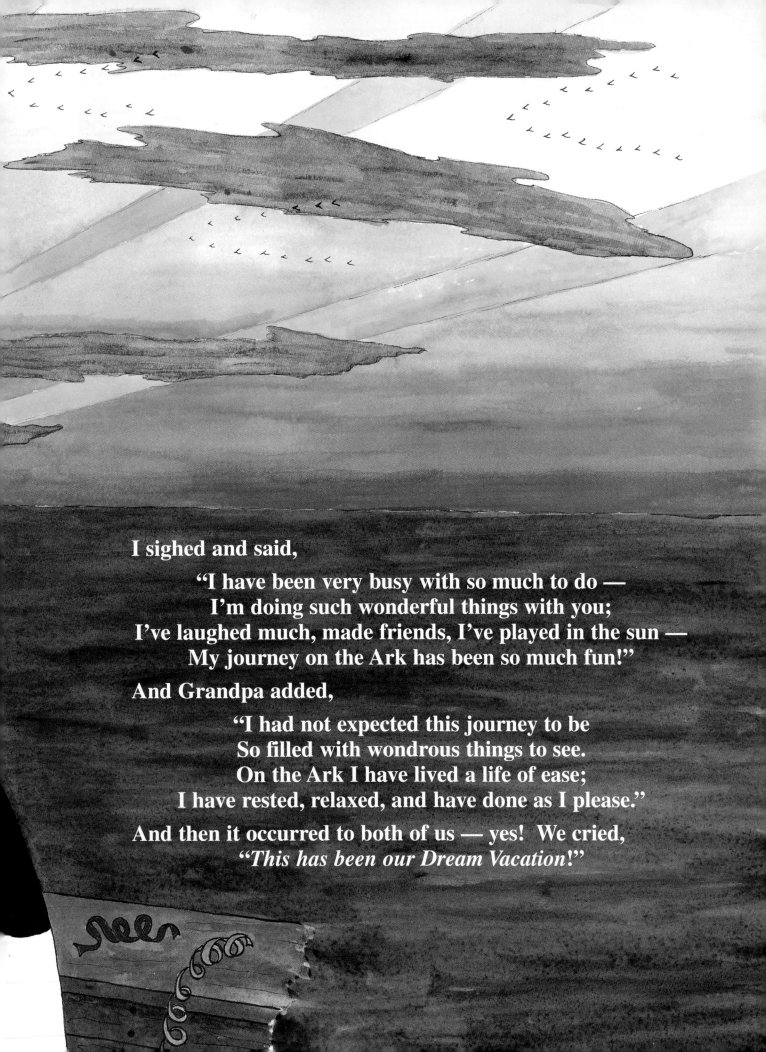

I sighed and said,

"I have been very busy with so much to do —
I'm doing such wonderful things with you;
I've laughed much, made friends, I've played in the sun —
My journey on the Ark has been so much fun!"

And Grandpa added,

"I had not expected this journey to be
So filled with wondrous things to see.
On the Ark I have lived a life of ease;
I have rested, relaxed, and have done as I please."

And then it occurred to both of us — yes! We cried,
"This has been our Dream Vacation!"

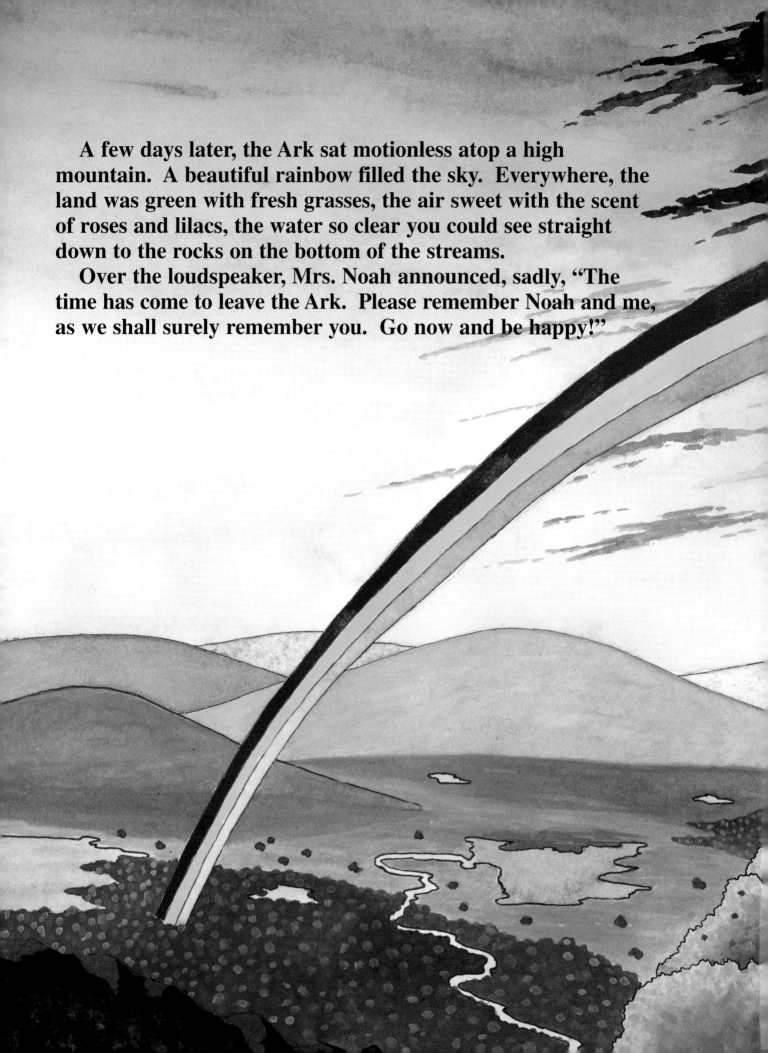

A few days later, the Ark sat motionless atop a high mountain. A beautiful rainbow filled the sky. Everywhere, the land was green with fresh grasses, the air sweet with the scent of roses and lilacs, the water so clear you could see straight down to the rocks on the bottom of the streams.

Over the loudspeaker, Mrs. Noah announced, sadly, "The time has come to leave the Ark. Please remember Noah and me, as we shall surely remember you. Go now and be happy!"